LISTEN CLOSELY. I ONLY HAVE *TIME* TO GO OVER THIS *ONCE*.

AS NEAR AS WE HERE AT THE *WEIRD HAPPENINGS* ORGANIZATION CAN TELL--

--THE MAN RESPONSIBLE FOR ALL OF THIS IS *DOCTOR JONOTHON CAYRE* ...

...A BRILLIANT *BIO-PHYSICIST.* HE'S THE *PORTRAIT* OF A *MAD SCIENTIST*--

--COMPLETE WITH A *DERANGED* LAB ASSISTANT.

"NORM" IS A *LIFE MODEL DECOY.* AN *L.M.D.* A *ROBOT.*

CAYRE *ACQUIRED* THE *L.M.D.* WHEN THE DOCTOR WAS WORKING WITH *MACHINESMITH* IN THE *STATES.*

YEARS AGO IN *AMERICA,* CAYRE WITNESSED A BATTLE BETWEEN *THOR* AND A *GALACTUS HERALD* KNOWN AS THE *AIR-WALKER.*

APPARENTLY *GALACTUS* BUILDS HIS ANDROIDS TO *LAST.*

THE AIR-WALKER CAME EQUIPPED WITH *SELF-REGENERATING* TECHNOLOGY.

CAYRE MANAGED TO GET HIS HANDS ON THE *SMALLEST PIECE* OF ALIEN DEBRIS--

I SUPPOSE IT'S UP TO **EXCALIBUR** TO VOLUNTEER!

"AND IN ENGLAND'S DARKEST HOURS...

"...EXCALIBUR, HER MIGHTY BLADE, WILL ONCE MORE BE DRAWN."

PARDON, BRIGADIER?

YES, SIR! TRACKING NOW...

I WASN'T TALKING TO YOU, PEEL!

BUT I AM WHEN I SAY I WANT YOU TO MONITOR THEIR EVERY MOVE!

LOSE TRACK OF THEM -- YOU'VE LOST YOUR JOB!

GOT IT, MISTER?

I WANT UPDATES EVERY FIVE MINUTES!

CHAPTER 2

YOU HAVE COME A *LONG WAY* FROM THE *CIRCUS, KURT WAGNER.*

THERE WAS A TIME WHEN YOUR *BIGGEST* CONCERN WAS SHARING A DRESSING ROOM WITH *GILDA* THE *BEARDED LADY.*

OPERATIVE: NIGHTCRAWLER.

ABILITY = TELEPORTER.

LOCATION = GLASGOW GALLERIA.

OBJECTIVE = DISARMING NUCLEAR WARHEAD DESIGNATED "NORM."

YEARS LATER, YOU'RE *PROWLING* ABOUT A CROWDED SHOPPING MALL IN GLASGOW IN SEARCH OF A WALKING *NUCLEAR WARHEAD!*

SUDDENLY, IT SEEMS *PETTY* TO HAVE COMPLAINED ABOUT *HAIR* IN THE *SINK.*

I MUST BE DISCREET.

ALERTING NORM TO MY PRESENCE WILL AVAIL ME NOTHING.

NOW TO--

WILL THAT BE ALL, MR.--?

YOU DON'T RECOGNIZE ME?

SHOULD I?

NEIN. GOOD.

MOMMY, THAT MAN HAS A TAIL!

DON'T POINT, DEAR. IT'S IMPOLITE.

'AT AIN'T NO MAN! IT'S NIGHTCRAWLER!

SO IT IS!

NICE TA MEET YA!

BRITAIN A JERK OR WHA--

PHOENIX'S PHONE NUMBER?

WHAT ARE YOU DOIN' HERE?

WOULD YOU BELIEVE, BEING DISCREET?

SO IT BEGINS.

YOUR INTENT IS TO NEUTRALIZE THIS UNIT.

YOU SEEK TO INTERROGATE ME TO GAIN INFORMATION REGARDING MASTER CAYRE'S PLANS!

TOUGH LUCK, NIGHTCRAWLER-- THIS UNIT'S NOT FOR DISSECTING!

WITH MY WIRING EXPOSED, I CANNOT *DISGUISE* MY APPEARANCE.

INTERNALLY INJURED AS I AM, I CANNOT *FIGHT* MY WAY TO SAFETY.

I *REFUSE* TO BE CAPTURED.

THEREFORE, I HAVE *ACTIVATED* MY *NUCLEAR WARHEAD.*

IN *THIRTY* SECONDS I WILL BUILD TO CRITICAL MASS.

TIK TIK TIK TIK TIK

JUST THOUGHT YOU'D LIKE TO KNOW.

THIRTY SECONDS?

PLENTY OF TIME.

WHERE'D THEY GO?

BAMF

WHAT'S THAT SMELL?

WHERE'S CAPTAIN BRIT?

DO THEY HAVE "BLUE LIGHT SPECIALS" IN ENGLAND?

BLUFFING ABOUT THE WARHEAD?

KREEAKT!

KRREE

KARR

RREEERR

I HOPE CAYRE SAVED HIS *WARRANTY* ON THIS *PROTOTYPE.*

WITH ANY LUCK, HE CAN TRADE IT IN FOR AN *ULTIMATE NULLIFIER* OR SOMETHING.

LET'S HEAR IT FOR THE LITTLE GIRL FROM *DEERFIELD, ILLINOIS!* IT TOOK ALL OF *TWELVE SECONDS* TO ACHIEVE MY OBJECTIVE.

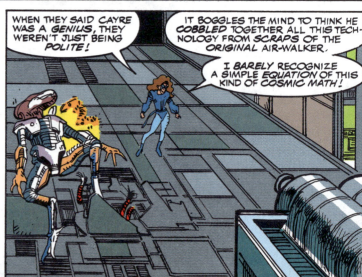

WHEN THEY SAID CAYRE WAS A *GENIUS,* THEY WEREN'T JUST BEING *POLITE!*

IT BOGGLES THE MIND TO THINK HE *COBBLED* TOGETHER ALL THIS TECHNOLOGY FROM *SCRAPS* OF THE ORIGINAL AIR-WALKER.

I BARELY RECOGNIZE A SIMPLE *EQUATION* OF THIS KIND OF *COSMIC MATH!*

MAYBE I CAN *AT LEAST* FIND "X."

BRING DOWN THE VARIABLE INTEGERS--

--CARRY THE THREE12Y...

...MULTIPLY BY-- A *CARROT?!*

pip

FACE IT, PRYDE.

YOU HAVEN'T...

...GOT...

...A...

...CLUE.

SO MUCH FOR THE JOYS OF TRIAL AND ERROR.

I *SHOULD* HAVE FIGURED --THE SAME WAY I CAN HOLD ONTO PEOPLE WHEN I'M PHASED...

...SIMILARLY ALTERED OBJECTS CAN HAVE A DIRECT EFFECT ON ME!

THE GOOD NEWS BEING--

--I DON'T HAVE TO SPEND THIS *ENTIRE* BATTLE ON THE DEFENSIVE!

I'M NOT A TEENAGE MUTANT *NINJA* FOR NOTHING!

KRREEEAKT!

THEN AGAIN--

--MAYBE IT *IS* ALL FOR NOTHING!

KREEEAKT!

RUB IT IN.

KRREEEAKT!

OH, SHUT UP.

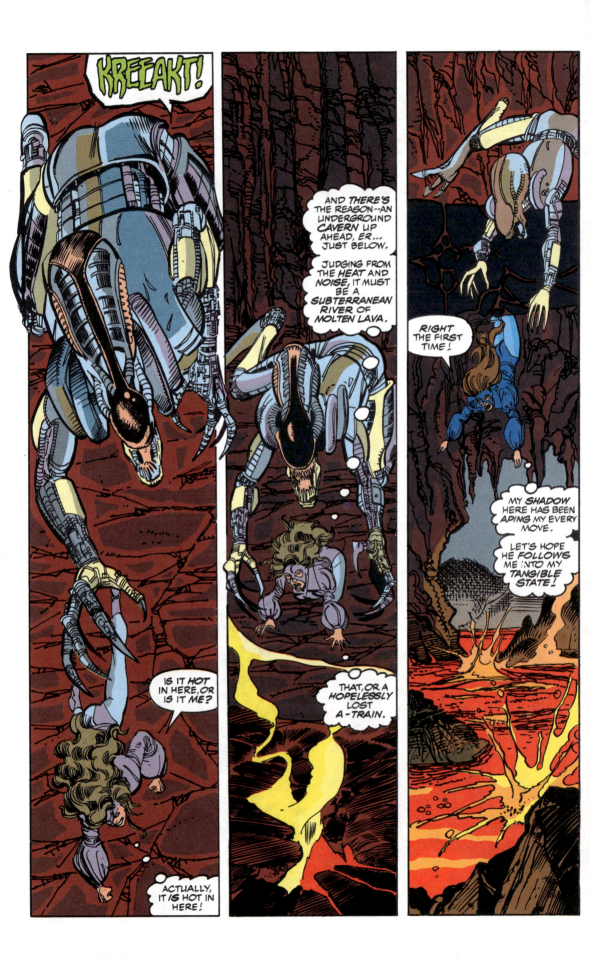

:GASP: Y-YOU'RE A ROBOT?!

ONLY HALF-ROBOT. THE REST IS THE REMAINS OF A U.S. SOLDIER NAMED ERIC SAVIN.

CORRECTION: THERE IS ACTUALLY A 79-TO-21% RATIO OF --

SHUT UP, COMPUTER.

SOMEBODY'S PAYING ME A LOT OF MONEY FOR CAYRE'S NOTES.

REALLY? I'M CURIOUS --

-- HOW MUCH DOES A CYBORG'S SOUL COST?

CHEAP SHOT, LADY.

THE LAST THING I NEED IS CAREER COUNSELING FROM A WOMAN WHOSE BODY IS COVERED IN SCALES.

NO MATTER HOW CONSIDERABLE THAT BODY MAY BE.

I WISH I HAD THE TIME -- AND THE WORDS -- TO CONVINCE YOU...

...BUT THE BOMB-THING I SET IS GOING TO GO OFF ANY MINUTE!

WARNING! MEGGAN IS ENGAGED IN *EVASIVE* ACTION!

TELL ME SOMETHING I *DON'T KNOW.*

THERE IS NOT ENOUGH *TIME* TO TELL YOU *EVERYTHING* YOU DON'T KNOW.

COMPUTER, PLEASE. LESS *SCHTICK* AND MORE ASSISTANCE!

WARNING! MEGGAN IS ASTRIDE YOUR *SHOULD*--

COMPUTER...?

SHUT UP?

LISTEN, MR.--?

COLDBLOOD.

--MR. *COLDBLOOD,* MY BOYFRIEND IS *REALLY REALLY* RICH.

IF I *PROMISE* TO GET HIM TO PAY *YOU MORE* MONEY THAN THESE *OTHER* PEOPLE--

--WOULD YOU HELP ME *DESTROY* ALL THE NOTES?

YOU'RE *KIDDING,* RIGHT?

I MAY BE NEW TO THIS *CYBORG-FOR-HIRE* VOCATION--

--BUT I'M SURE THAT'S *ONE* WAY TO GET KICKED OUT OF THE *PROFESSIONAL MERCENARY'S* GUILD.

{UNH}

QUERY? DID YOU *MEAN* TO USE *EXCESSIVE* FORCE?

ANOTHER CHEAP SHOT, LADY.

YOU PLAY OFF MY *SELF-HATRED* OVER BEING HALF-DEAD, HALF-ROBOT...

...AND I *FORSAKE* MY MILLION-DOLLAR DEAL?

LIKE I'M GOING TO FLUSH MY *FIRST MERC CONTRACT* DOWN THE DRAIN--

--JUST TO SAVE THE WORLD.

UNLIKELY.

YOU MAY *LOOK* LIKE A BIMBO-- BUT YOU'RE REALLY A *SHREWD ONE,* MEGGAN.

I DON'T MEAN TO LOOK LIKE A "BIMBO!"

GET *OUT OF* HERE, KID.

QUERY-- WHAT ARE YOU *DOING?!*

WHAT DOES IT *LOOK* LIKE?

THAT YOU'RE "*GOING* TO *FLUSH OUR* FIRST MERC CONTRACT DOWN THE DRAIN--

--JUST TO SAVE THE WORLD."

EXACTLY.

WRRRIIP

BUT I *CAN'T* LEAVE, YET! I HAVE TO PUT IN THE VIRUS TO DESTROY ALL HIS NOTES...

...BEFORE THE NEXT *SIXTY SECONDS* WHEN THIS LAB EXPLODES.

I'M ON IT!

THIS IS *NO WAY* TO ESTABLISH A *RESUMÉ* CONDUCIVE TO--

SHUT UP, COMPUTER! JUST *CONFIRM* THAT I'M *SPLICING TOGETHER* THE PROPER WIRES.

CONFIRMED. VIRUS INITIATED THROUGH-OUT SYSTEM.

BUT GLASS...?

GLASS IS AN ENTIRELY DIFFERENT MATTER!

A WASTE OF TIME! EVEN IF THE GLASS SHARDS KILL ME--I'LL ONLY RESURRECT MYSELF!

WHO SAID ANYTHING ABOUT KILLING YOU?

I'M USING THE PHOENIX POWER TO FORGE IT ALL INTO AN AIRTIGHT CHRYSALIS.

BUT, I C-CAN'T BREATHE! I'LL...

DIE. AND RESURRECT.

AND DIE. AND RESURRECT. BUT AT LEAST ALL YOUR MOLECULES ARE IN ONE PLACE.

WITH ANY LUCK AT ALL, THESE W.H.O. TECHS MIGHT BE ABLE TO CURE YOU SOMEDAY.

AND SOMEDAY AFTER THAT--YOU MIGHT BE ABLE TO FORGIVE YOURSELF FOR ALL YOU'VE DONE.

I KNOW I NEVER WILL.

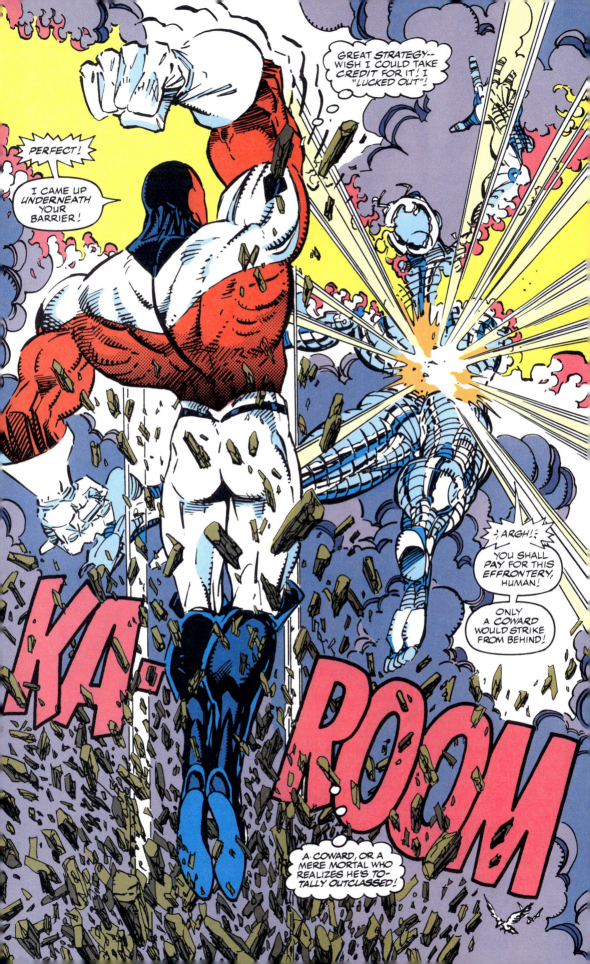

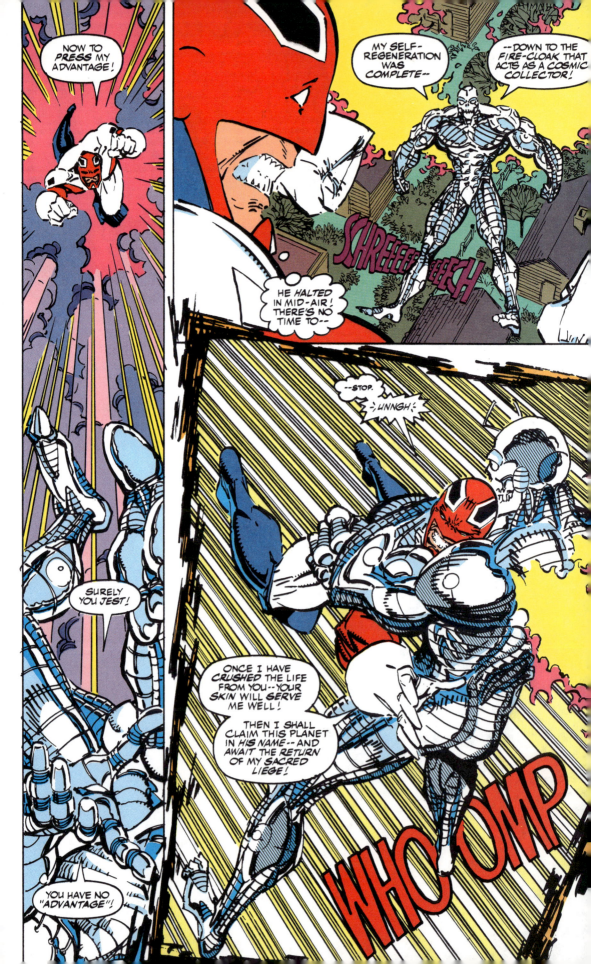

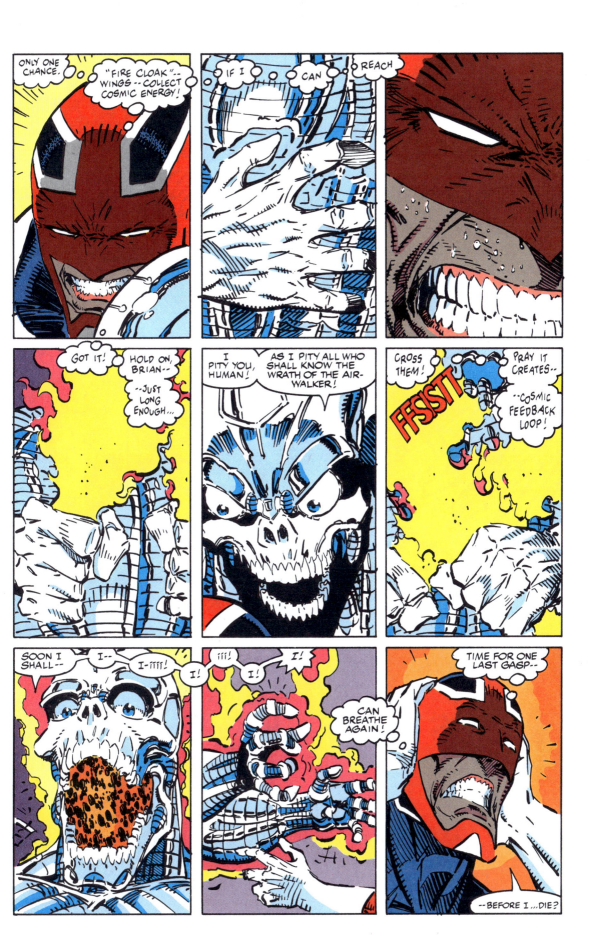

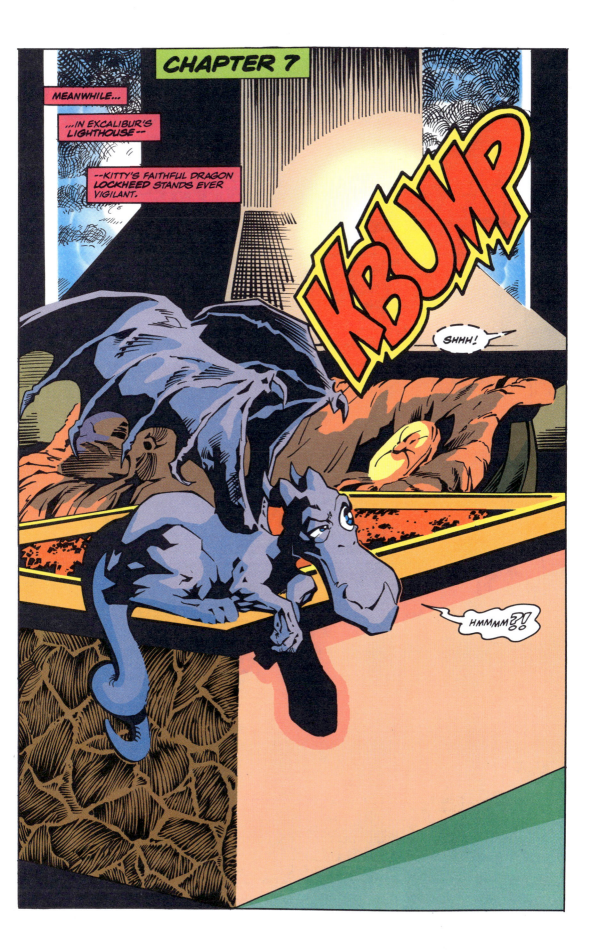

IT'S A GHOST!

AAAAIIIEEE!

THERE'S ANOTHER WORD YOU READ A *LOT*, BUT NEVER REALLY GET TO USE.

HIHH HIHH HIHH

HIH HE

HEE HEE HEE

HEE HEE HEE HEE HEE HEE HEE HEE HEE HEE HEE HEE HEE HEE HEE HEE HEE HEE HEE HEE HEE HEE HEE HEE HEE HEE HEE HEE

!!!

WHO WAS THE *LAST* ONE OUT THIS MORNING?!

THAT WAS *ME*. BUT I'M *SURE* I CLOSED THE DOOR.

HMMP...

A STRONG WIND, PERHAPS, MEIN FREUND?